Off Off Broadway Festival Plays

38th Series

DANCING TURTLE
by Thomas M. Atkinson

FRISKY & THE PANDA MAN
by Ross Howard

OLD FLAME
by Mira Gibson

REALITY PLAY
by Mark Swaner

TATTOO YOU
by Lisa Kenner Grissom

TORNADO
by Arlitia Jones

A SAMUEL FRENCH ACTING EDITION

SAMUEL FRENCH

FOUNDED 1830

SAMUELFRENCH.COM
SAMUELFRENCH-LONDON.CO.UK

PLAY

ISBN 978-0-573-70217-4

www.SamuelFrench.com
www.SamuelFrench-London.co.uk

FOR PRODUCTION ENQUIRIES

UNITED STATES AND CANADA
Info@SamuelFrench.com
1-866-598-8449

UNITED KINGDOM AND EUROPE
Plays@SamuelFrench-London.co.uk
020-7255-4302

Each title is subject to availability from Samuel French, depending upon country of performance. Please be aware that *DANCING TURTLE, FRISKY & THE PANDA MAN, OLD FLAME, REALITY PLAY, TATTOO YOU,* and *TORNADO* may not be licensed by Samuel French in your territory. Professional and amateur producers should contact the nearest Samuel French office or licensing partner to verify availability.

CAUTION: Professional and amateur producers are hereby warned that *DANCING TURTLE, FRISKY & THE PANDA MAN, OLD FLAME, REALITY PLAY, TATTOO YOU,* and *TORNADO* are subject to a licensing fee. Publication of this play(s) does not imply availability for performance. Both amateurs and professionals considering a production are strongly advised to apply to Samuel French before starting rehearsals, advertising, or booking a theatre. A licensing fee must be paid whether the title(s) is presented for charity or gain and whether or not admission is charged. Professional/Stock licensing fees are quoted upon application to Samuel French.

No one shall make any changes in this title(s) for the purpose of production. No part of this book may be reproduced, stored in a retrieval system, or transmitted in any form, by any means, now known or yet to be invented, including mechanical, electronic, photocopying, recording, videotaping, or otherwise, without the prior written permission of the publisher. No one shall upload this title(s), or part of this title(s), to any social media websites.

For all enquiries regarding motion picture, television, and other media rights, please contact Samuel French.

MUSIC USE NOTE

Licensees are solely responsible for obtaining formal written permission from copyright owners to use copyrighted music in the performance of this play and are strongly cautioned to do so. If no such permission is obtained by the licensee, then the licensee must use only original music that the licensee owns and controls. Licensees are solely responsible and liable for all music clearances and shall indemnify the copyright owners of the play(s) and their licensing agent, Samuel French, against any costs, expenses, losses and liabilities arising from the use of music by licensees. Please contact the appropriate music licensing authority in your territory for the rights to any incidental music.

IMPORTANT BILLING AND CREDIT REQUIREMENTS

If you have obtained performance rights to this title, please refer to your licensing agreement for important billing and credit requirements.

The Samuel French Off Off Broadway Short Play Festival started in 1975 and is one of the nation's most established and highly regarded short play festivals. During the course of the Festival's 38 years, over 500 theatre companies and schools participated in the Festival, including companies from coast to coast as well as abroad from Canada, Singapore, and the United Kingdom. Over the years, more than 200 submitted plays have been published, with many of the participants becoming established, award-winning playwrights.

Festival Coordinator: Billie Davis
Production Coordinator: Casey McLain
Literary Coordinator: Amy Rose Marsh
Associate Literary Coordinator: Katie Lupica
Marketing Coordinator: Katy DiSavino
Associate Marketing Coordinator: Alison Sundstrom
Judge Coordinator: Abbie Van Nostrand
Graphic Design: Gene Sweeney
House Manager: Tyler Mullen
Production Assistant: Ben Coleman
Executive Director: Bruce Lazarus
Festival Interns: Ariana Callan, Ashley Belle, Gwyndolyn Ballard, Jordan Sucher, and Sarah Weber
Festival Staff: Matthew Akers, Eric Beauzay, Nate Collins, Ken Dingledine, Joe Ferreira, Joe Garner, Alicia Grey, Glenn Halcomb, Laura Lindson, Chris Lonstrup, Dora Naughton, Fred Schnitzer, Charlie Sou, and Jordon Villines

GUEST JUDGES

Charles Busch
Jack Cummings III
Jason Eagan
Amanda Green
Julie Halston
Anne Kaufman
Emily Morse
Tim Pinckney
Connie Ray
Ken Rus Schmoll
Jenny Schwartz
Keala Settle

For more information on the Samuel French Off Off Broadway Short Play Festival, including history, interviews, and more, please visit www.oob.samuelfrench.com.

CONTENTS

Dancing Turtle

Thomas M. Atkinson

DANCING TURTLE received its premiere production at the inaugural 2012 Piper Plays: Smart Plays for Young Actors Festival in Brooklyn where it took 1st place. It was directed by Rachel Rear. The cast was as follows:

MOLLY . . . . Justice Buckmaster

MARY, INDIAN DANCER #1 . . . . Rosalind Lilly

MOTHER, GIFT SHOP CLERK, INDIAN DANCER #2 . . . . Elisa Blynn

INDIAN BOY, FATHER. . . . . Tim Ling

DANCING TURTLE was produced as part of the 38th Annual Samuel French Off Off Broadway Short Play Festival at the Clurman Theater at Theater Row in New York City on July 26, 2013. It was directed by Rachel Rear. The cast was as follows:

MOLLY . . . . Justice Buckmaster

MARY, INDIAN DANCER #1 . . . . Rosalind Lilly

MOTHER, GIFT SHOP CLERK, INDIAN DANCER #2 . . . . Rachel Rear

INDIAN BOY, FATHER. . . . . Shahar Isaac Katz

CHARACTERS

MOLLY – female, perhaps 16 or 17, severely wracked by cerebral palsy, wearing a small, beaded leather bag around her neck

MARY – (also **INDIAN DANCER #1**) female, perhaps 20, Molly's beautiful, idealized, elegant, articulate version of herself

MOTHER – (also **GIFT SHOP CLERK** and **INDIAN DANCER #2**) female, 40-45, Molly's mother

INDIAN BOY – (also **FATHER**) male, American Indian, 15-20, with long hair

SET

The stage should be empty except for a slatted park bench with a blue Rollator (a combination walker wheelchair) behind it.

PROPERTY PLOT

Canvas carry-all purse for **MOTHER**
Hide-covered Cottonwood drum for **INDIAN BOY** in final scene.

COSTUMES

MOLLY – Molly is dressed in jeans, an old t-shirt, and practical athletic shoes. Her clothes are worn but clean and cared for. She wears a small beaded leather bag around her neck.

MARY – Mary is dressed in a simple, white gown, with no shoes. She is unadorned by jewelry, accessories or make-up. Her change to **INDIAN DANCER #1** is implied, and no costume change should take place.

MOTHER – Mother is dressed like Molly, but with an open, unbuttoned plaid shirt. She also has a large, canvas carry-all purse.

As **GIFT SHOP CLERK**, she slips on a smock and bandana (inside the carry-all purse), which can come on and off quickly.

As **INDIAN DANCER #2**, she slips on a beaded leather vest, also a change which can happen quickly.

INDIAN BOY – Indian Boy wears boots, jeans, and a blood red Western pearl-button shirt. He is wearing an elaborate white bone hair-pipe breastplate necklace and his long hair is down.

As **FATHER** his hair is tucked up under a camouflage baseball cap, and his shirt and necklace are hidden by a zipped-up Carhartt work jacket.

ABOUT THE PLAYWRIGHT

Thomas M. Atkinson is an author and playwright, current 2014 Ohio Arts Council Individual Excellence award winner, and the 2013 OAC/Fine Arts Work Center Writer-in-Residence in Provincetown, MA. Some of his full-length plays include: *Clear Liquor & Coal Black Nights* (Playhouse in the Park), *Copperheads* (Ensemble Theatre of Cincinnati), and *Cuttings* (ETC, Theatre Conspiracy, Culture Park Theatre). His short plays include *Dancing Turtle* and *Battling the Ghost of Max Schmeling*, which was one of seven winners (out of 583 entries from 38 states and 8 countries), and performed at Fusion Theatre's 2014 THE SEVEN: Worlds Collide Festival in Albuquerque, NM. His short fiction has appeared in *The Sun, The North American Review, The Indiana Review, The Tampa Review, Fifth Wednesday Journal, The Moon, City Beat* and *Electron Press Magazine.* His short story, "Grimace in the Burnt Black Hills," received two separate Pushcart Prize nominations after appearing in *The Sun* magazine. His first novel, *Strobe Life,* is currently available on Amazon for Kindle, and he has just completed his second novel, *Tiki Man,* which was selected as one of four finalists for the 2014 Leapfrog Press Fiction Contest. He has won numerous honors and awards for both fiction and drama, including five Ohio Arts Council grants. He lives in southwest Ohio with his wife and two sons.

(Morning. The bench is the front seat of a car. **MOTHER** *is driving.* **MOLLY** *is in the passenger seat – her body twisted painfully by cerebral palsy, most obviously in her neck, wrists and hands.* **MARY** *appears from the darkness behind* **MOLLY** *and gently places her hands on* **MOLLY** *'s shoulders.* **MOLLY** *doesn't react.)*

MARY. Mom's taking me to the Appalachian Festival today, almost to Cincinnati, along the river. Dad's staying home to move the bars up in the bathroom. We drop down and take Route 32 - "The James A. Rhodes AppalachianHighway" - for the better part of two hours. And when we pass the sign for Burnt Cabin Road, Mom says, like she always does,

MOTHER. There's a story there.

*(***MOLLY** *smiles, which looks much like a grimace.)*

MARY. She points out stands of corn and fall-down barns, and every so often she turns to me and says,

MOTHER. Molly, need to stop?

MOLLY. Nnnn!

MARY. That's the sound I make that we all know means "no." Like a wheel bearing going bad Dad says, if a wheel bearing going bad starts with an "N."

(strokes **MOLLY** *'s hair)*

Holding my bladder has become something of a point of pride for me these last three years since, due to some difficulties during my birth, potty training ended and menstruation began in the very same month.

MOTHER. Here we are!

*(***MOTHER** *turns and gets up from the bench like it's a car seat. She starts fussing behind the bench with the Rollator.* **MOLLY** *shakes her head "no.")*

MARY. It's bad enough parking up front in a blue sign space, but my *stupid* Rollator.

*(considers the Rollator as **MOTHER** wheels it out from behind **MOLLY**'s side of the bench)*

It's a walker with wheels and a little seat with a wire basket underneath and bicycle brakes that I can't use very well any way. I'd rather just walk my walk. An Indian doctor at Children's -an India Indian, not an American Indian- he told my dad it might help and that's all it took. Twelve hours of price shopping on the internet later, I'm the not-so-proud owner of a shiny blue Medline Rollator with eight inch wheels to give me "confidence on all terrains." At least it's not the pink "Breast Cancer Awareness" model. I think he was expecting more.

MOLLY. *(shaking her head "No")* Geez nat aids.

MARY. *(translating)* Geezers and fat ladies.

MOTHER. *(smiling)* Are you sure? I told you, there's going to be a lot of walking.

*(**MOTHER** shrugs her shoulders and leans in to help **MOLLY** out. **INDIAN BOY** enters. **INDIAN BOY** and **MARY** perform an elegant pas de deux as **MOTHER** struggles helping **MOLLY** up.)*

MARY. She slips her arms around me, her face warm in my neck, waiting for the touch of my twisted hands against her back. It's a dance we've done a million times, and the only graceful moment of my day. And sometimes, in that brief stillness before she says,

MOTHER. Ready?

MARY. I pretend she's a boy.

*(**MOTHER** holds **MOLLY** for a moment, then lets her lean against the Rollator to rest. **INDIAN BOY** exits.)*

MARY. It never happens with my dad because he still makes fart noises against my neck like he did when I was little. Then I act like I'm mad and he acts like he believes me.

(**MOTHER** *fusses in a large canvas carry-all.*)

MOTHER. (*pretending, badly, that she's just thought of it*) You know, I might just bring it for me. I can hang my bag on the handle and the little basket can hold all the crap your father's so rightly worried we're going to buy.

(**MOLLY** *and* **MARY** *both look at the little basket.*)

MARY. I hate that little basket.

(**MOTHER** *and* **MOLLY** *begin walking slowly around the stage.* **MOTHER** *is pushing the Rollator.* **MOLLY***'s gait is awkward and unbalanced and painful to watch.* **MARY** *shadows her at a short distance.*)

(*SOUND CUE #1: Indistinct festival crowd sounds, distant bluegrass music*)

(**MOLLY, MOTHER** *and* **MARY** *look around at the imagined festival going on around them.*)

MARY. (*looking around*) There are men dressed up like pioneers with tall boots and string-laced shirts and women with loose skirts and bonnets. And Indians. More Indians than I've ever seen in one place. Some are in costumes and feathers and war paint, but most are just in their everyday clothes. And there's a boy,

(*SOUND CUE #2: Festival sounds fade out*)

(**INDIAN BOY** *enters and crosses the stage dressed in new jeans and a red western shirt with pearl buttons. His hair is long and black and he is wearing a white bone hair-pipe breastplate necklace.* **MOLLY** *tries to smile at him.* **MARY** *flashes him a dazzling smile. He nods in their direction, but may well be acknowledging someone else.* **INDIAN BOY** *exits.*)

MARY. There's Indians out our way too, the United Remnant Band of the Shawnee Nation. They're supposed to be what's left of the Shawnee that wouldn't move out West when Tecumseh died, and after all this time a lot of them don't look much like Indians.

(**INDIAN BOY** *enters as* **FATHER**, *dressed in a stained Carhartt jacket and a camouflage hunting cap.* **MOLLY** *takes the Rollator and he leads her gently by the elbow.* **MOTHER** *puts on the smock and bandana and goes to stand behind the bench as if it is a counter, becoming* **GIFT SHOP CLERK**. **MARY** *continues to shadow* **MOLLY**.)

MARY. They run a little cavern and Dad took me last Spring. It was hard to get around and I didn't much like it in there, eight inch wheels or not. In the little museum, he stared at a stuffed buffalo head on the wall for a long time, and then he said,

FATHER. *(turning to* **MOLLY***)* Beats the other end sticking out of the wall!

(**MOLLY** *smiles.*)

MARY. He hunts, but I don't think he'd put any heads on our wall even if Mom let him. He hunts deer and wild turkey mostly. He used to hunt squirrel and rabbit too, until he brought home a little rabbit once and I cried and cried. The deer and turkey are all dressed-out and wrapped in white butcher's paper by the time I see them, and once I tried venison breakfast sausage, I won't eat anything else.

(**FATHER** *and* **MOLLY** *look down at the bench as if it's a glass display counter.* **MOLLY** *points awkwardly.*)

MARY. In the gift shop, I wanted a tomahawk with a heart cut out of the black blade.

FATHER. *(smiling)* Good try. How about that little leather sidebag? I'll get some of these 'dreamcatcher' earrings for your Mother.

MOLLY. Ill ate ohs!

MARY. She'll hate those!

FATHER. *(smiling)* Yeah? Let's see!

(**FATHER** *pays* GIFT SHOP CLERK, *and she gives* **FATHER** *an exaggerated sympathetic smile.*)

MARY. And that heavy-set woman behind the counter gave him one of those looks, the one I always think they should wait and give when I'm not in the room. Or at least not looking right at them.

(FATHER *visibly stiffens. He counts his change and takes imagined bag. He guides* MOLLY *away from the bench. He motions with his head back at* GIFT SHOP CLERK.)

FATHER. *(loudly)* Indian Princess "Eats Many Fry Bread."

(MOLLY *smiles.* GIFT SHOP CLERK *grimaces.*)

MARY. Dad doesn't deal very well with my public.

(GIFT SHOP CLERK *comes from behind the bench and removes smock and bandana, becoming* MOTHER *again.* FATHER *delivers* MOLLY *to her care and exits.* MOTHER *takes over the Rollator.*)

Mom hates those earrings, and whenever we need a laugh, he makes her to put them on.

(MOLLY *fusses with the small, beaded leather bag around her neck.*)

Do you know what's in there? Four white shells from our trip to my uncle's in Florida, a Blue Jay feather and some eight-sided salt crystals big as dice. And a brass shell casing from when they shot off seven rifles at my grandfather's funeral.

(SOUND CUE 3#: *Three volleys of seven rifles*)

(*She and* MOTHER, MOLLY *stop to watch some imagined people go by.*)

A group of Indian women pass by. And I say,

MOLLY. Errr...near ins.

(MOTHER *puzzles for a moment, trying to suss out what* MOLLY *has said.*)

MOTHER. *(smiling)* My earrings? The dreamcatchers? *Those* ugly things? Yeah, looks like I should have worn them today. What *was* your father thinking?

(While MARY speaks, she, MOLLY and MOTHER walk slowly around the stage stopping occasionally.)

(SOUND CUE #4: Indistinct festival crowd sounds, distant bluegrass music)

MARY. We watch a blacksmith and listen to a bluegrass band. An old man with a long, grey beard makes rocking chairs all by hand, and a woman with bad teeth is weaving round baskets she says are from Scotland. Two little black girls in matching dresses dip string in warm beeswax to make candles. Sometimes my mind gets caught,

(SOUND CUE #5: Festival sounds fade out to a low, barely audible hum)

(MOLLY stops and stares at something intently until MOTHER speaks.)

MARY. *(watching what MOLLY is watching)* Like watching that blacksmith blow those orange coals almost white, or watching those candles get bigger without ever *seeing* them get bigger, or that old man stripping bark with a drawknife.

Then Mom or Dad has to break my line of sight, just for a second. And when she gets between me and those candles, she says,

MOTHER. Do you smell kettle corn?

(SOUND CUE #6: Low hum stops)

(MOLLY looks at MOTHER, startled from her study.)

MARY. Mom is crazy about kettle corn. And judging from the line, so is everyone else in Ohio, Kentucky and West Virginia.

MOTHER. What do you think? Half a bag or full? Can we eat a bag of kettle corn as long as your leg?

(sniffs the air)

Seems a shame to come all this way for *half* a bag. We can always take a bite or two home to your father.

(looks around)

Let's find you a place to sit.

*(**MARY** moves the bench and stands it on end backstage left, where it becomes the sugar maple tree. **MOTHER** guides **MOLLY** over to the bench. **MARY** and **MOTHER** help **MOLLY** sit on the stage floor in front of the bench.)*

MARY. We found me a nice spot under a sugar maple, not too close to the families picnicking with small children, on the edge of a big field with a tent at the center.

*(**MOTHER** parks the Rollator behind the bench, then shields her eyes and scans the audience.)*

MOTHER. Whew, that's a long line. But hey, kettle corn is kettle corn. If I'm not back by sundown, start crawling for the car.

*(**MOLLY** smiles and **MOTHER** exits. **MOLLY** arranges herself awkwardly in front of the bench.)*

MARY. "All akimbo" is how I would describe me sitting on the ground. As a matter of fact, it's probably how I would describe me. I love that word, "akimbo." I love the sound of it coming out of someone else's mouth. Once Dad found out, he uses it all the time. He says "a kimbo" is a Japanese knife they sell on the Home Shopping Channel.

*(**MOLLY** begins staring intently at the ground right in front of her.)*

(SOUND CUE #7: Low, barely audible hum starts)

MARY. I get caught by a little ribbon of red cellophane, like from a cigarette pack, waving in the gentle breeze like a tiny banner on a flagpole of grass.

The PA system crackles an announcement, but I'm not paying attention.

(SOUND CUE #8: Low hum fades out as the sound of Native American drumming begins - the even pulse of a drum circle playing a hide-covered cottonwood drum)

(**MOLLY** *looks up.*)

MARY. When the drumming starts I *feel* it, feel it in the ground, right up through my seat. Indian drums. And even though I can see them banging on stretched hide, gathered around that little tent, the vibrations seem like they're from far, far away.

(**INDIAN BOY** *enters with a cottonwood drum and stands center stage. He begins drumming and a chanting song that continues until almost the end of the play.*)

INDIAN BOY. (*sings an intertribal song – vocable, non-language syllables*) Ah Hey Yah Ho. Ah Hey Yah Ho.

MARY. His song has no words, just vowels and repeated syllables, droning low notes that are achingly familiar.

(**MOTHER** *enters wearing beaded leather vest and begins a slow shuffling dance around* **INDIAN BOY.**)

MARY. Two women in deerskin dresses begin a slow shuffling dance in a wide circle around him. Other Indians fall in behind them and as they stagger-step around the field, they motion for everyone to join them. Mostly it's little kids that do, little blond boys and girls looking for any excuse to run around. But there's something about the dance, the awkward hesitant rhythm of it, that reaches right inside me. I call to those two women.

MOLLY. (*painfully, earnestly*) Uhnnn! Uhnnn!

MARY. And for the first time in my life, I know it doesn't matter if I sound like the honking of a goose on the wing.

(**MOLLY** *falls on her side trying to get herself up.* **MARY** *kneels beside her, willing her on.*)

MARY. I fall over trying to get myself up, because I know, I *know* that I have to be out there.

(**MOLLY** *rolls onto her stomach and struggles in vain to push herself up.*)

MARY. And as I battle my unforgiving body, two worn and beaded moccasins appear at each elbow.

(**MOTHER** *and* **MARY** *help lift up* **MOLLY**. *They ease her slowly into the dancing circle around* **INDIAN BOY**.)

MARY. They lift me up, cooing comfort, the deerskin soft as velvet against my arms. We work our way into the slow current of dancers, floating down like autumn leaves into that song. And when they finally let go,

(**MOTHER** *and* **MARY** *let go of* **MOLLY**. **MOLLY** *does her awkward version of a stomp dance and* **MOTHER** *and* **MARY** *dance in line behind her.*)

MARY. I'm out in front, and everyone behind follows my skewed path, heads down and halting steps, to somewhere I've never been. I don't know how long his song goes on, or how many times I pass close by the boy in the bone necklace, close enough it seems to me, to feel the breath of it on my cheek. I only know that I live another life, that for the length of it the pain is gone, gone like it had never been, gone like the lost ghost of a memory.

(**MOTHER** *exits.* **INDIAN BOY** *finishes his song.*)

(*SOUND CUE #9: Native American drumming fades out*)

(**MOLLY** *stops in front of him. She continues dancing in place while she stares at him.* **MARY** *dances in place behind her.*)

MARY. And when it's over, I shuffle in place before him, my eyes, fixed in the erratic orbit of my head, locked on to his. I say,

MOLLY. Eye nnn ur art!

(**INDIAN BOY** *cannot understand her.* **MARY** *stands close behind* **MOLLY**.)

MARY. "I can hear your heart."

(**INDIAN BOY** *smiles, but looks past her to search for who is supposed to be taking care of her.* **MOLLY** *continues to dance in place.*)

MARY. He smiles, and then cocks his head to look past my ear, searching for my keeper.

MOLLY. *(singing and dancing)* Eye nnn ur art!

(**INDIAN BOY** *exits.*)

MARY. I try to sing it, still dancing at his feet, knowing the words are lost, knowing all he can hear is the awful music of my voice, like some small thing, caught in the fine wire of a snare.

(**MARY** *holds* **MOLLY** *from behind, resting her head against* **MOLLY**'s *back.*)

(*Lights to black.*)

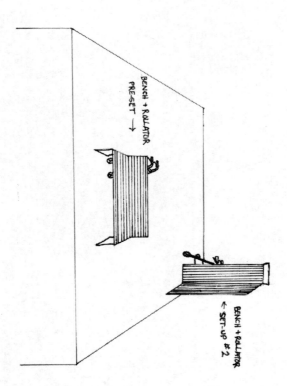

DANCING TURTLE
THOMAS N. ATKINSON

BENCH + ROLLATOR
PRE-SET →

BENCH + ROLLATOR
← SET-UP #2

Frisky & The Panda Man

Ross Howard

FRISKY & THE PANDA MAN was produced by the New Light Theatre Project (Sarah Norris, Artistic Director) as part of the 38th Annual Samuel French Off Off Broadway Short Play Festival at the Clurman Theater at Theater Row in New York City on July 25, 2013. The Director was Sarah Norris and the Production Stage Manager was Veronica Lee. The cast was as follows:

DR. OGDEN . . . . Chris Ryan

FRISKY . . . . Amanda Berry

INTERVIEWER . . . . Sarah Girard

CHARACTERS

DR. OGDEN – male. A slightly anxious panda conservationist.

FRISKY – female. A panda personified. She is the last panda in existence and appears to be a little "under the weather". She still does panda things like pandas do, if a little gingerly.

INTERVIEWER – female. Occupied with her phone or computer tablet throughout. Does not speak.

SCENE

A panda enclosure.

ABOUT THE PLAYWRIGHT

Ross Howard's plays have received full productions notably in London (Theatre 503, Upstairs at the Gatehouse, Riverside Studios, Old Red Lion), Las Vegas (Las Vegas Little Theatre, Onyx Theatre), Minneapolis (Pillsbury House Theatre), San Francisco (The Phoenix Theatre), and New York City (Cherry Lane Theatre, The Clurman Theatre). Hailing from Lancashire, in 2008 he was awarded a Playwright Fellowship from the Edward Albee Foundation. *Arthur and Esther* was awarded "Best of Fringe" at Las Vegas Fringe Festival 2010. *No One Loves Us Here* was a finalist for the New York Stage and Film Founders Award 2012, while *Frisky & The Panda Man* was a winning finalist in the 38th Samuel French Off Off Broadway Short Play Festival in 2013. Ross holds an M.F.A in playwriting from UNLV and has taught theatre and playwriting as an adjunct faculty member of the CSU Fresno theatre department. He is the current resident playwright of New Light Theater Project and now lives in London.

DR OGDEN. ...well we can all do a little more when it comes to the environment certainly. *(a beat)* But yes, like most people I got into animal conservation for the women. To be frank. At the start. For the ladies mainly. Animals, pandas, well all that came into my focus soon after. They have that effect on you. And Frisky here, well there she is. Just the one panda left. The last peanut in the bowl. She looks, well, "peaky" as you can see. This is how it is now. This is the situation. *(a beat)* Is all of this okay, so far?

INTERVIEWER. . . . . .

DR OGDEN. Anyway, that's a summary. Your hair looks great by the way.

INTERVIEWER. . . . . .

DR OGDEN. I also banged my funny bone on the gate coming in here. I can still feel it now. *(laughs)* It really hurts! *(a beat)* Anyway, I guess we're not here for small talk. And you've come a long way. This is a big interview, isn't it? A big deal... The end. Yes?

INTERVIEWER. . . . . .

DR OGDEN. If I hadn't been a conservationist? Are you wondering that? Now there's a question. Well, it's funny but between you and me, human to human, and Frisky won't mind hearing this, but underwater photography would have been where I'd have liked to have devoted more of my time. Or any time really. I mean, I haven't ever actually spent a single second doing it. But whenever I've seen pictures of things underwater, and it could be anything at all, fish or old shipwrecks, coral, I always hold my breath and think "Gosh. Look at that". But that's a whole other world isn't it? Under the ocean, I mean...?

INTERVIEWER. . . . .

(**DR OGDEN** *watches* **FRISKY** *eat bamboo.*)

DR OGDEN. I do sometimes wonder— sorry? Oh sorry, I thought you said something. Sorry. Yes, I do sometimes wonder if I'd have been happier in my adult life not pandering to pandas like I have. Not spending my days getting them to fuck at least! *(laughs and then stops)* Sorry, I don't mean to be crude, but that's really been the meat and potatoes of it these last few years. Getting them to have sex. So to speak. Mate. But yes, the seabed. That watery underworld. A secret world. Well it's something else I could have pursued instead certainly. I can imagine myself doing that. Snapping away with my camera. Wearing a snorkel...flippers... it must be so quiet...coming up to the surface, all that ocean spray. That, or maybe something to do with space. The vast solar system. *(A beat)* Do you want me to just keep going?

INTERVIEWER. . . . . .

DR OGDEN. It's not to say I haven't been fulfilled. I've travelled the world. Funny, I always resisted living in London for the longest time. Just thought it was over populated, and I'm not really one for weaving in and out of crowds of people as I'm walking along the pavement. Saying that, when I got the offer from Beijing I was off like a shot. So...well, I don't know... actually, can you just leave that bit out? I may come back to that, it's not very consistent...

INTERVIEWER. . . . . .

DR OGDEN. *(approaching* **FRISKY***)* Yes, it's been an awesome responsibility, I don't mind telling you. *(A beat)* Have you ever been in love? Hurts like hell, doesn't it? Oh well, here's a memory: I won an award and did some lectures some place for a month. Astrid, a woman, came to visit me on my second weekend there. We'd only been seeing each other every day for three weeks. It burned so bright between she and I. That first night of her visit, we made love four, five, six, five, times through the night, in between we just talked. She made me laugh and vice versa. It was lovely. It was warm, we sucked on ice lollies and went through a whole box. There was a dog. Every now and then we could hear its footsteps on the ceramic tile and its collar jingling outside our door. We smoked cigarettes and drank bottles of beer. We'd get up to brush our teeth together and come back to bed to kiss again. Neither of us could sleep because we loved each other so much. We couldn't believe our luck. She had a beautiful back. Summer breezes still remind me of her. We later took a trip across Europe, we went to Genoa, on the coast, I did most of the driving, all of it in actual fact, she didn't have a licence. When I opened the car door for her, she would get in and reach over and unlock my door as I was walking round. That's when you know you have a good one and should probably marry her. She made me see the stars. Life's remarkable. I said to myself "enjoy this while it lasts". It didn't last. Nothing does. Genoa. I wish we had our photograph taken. *(turns back to* **INTERVIEWER***)* Sorry, I don't know where I was — sorry...

INTERVIEWER. . . . . .

DR OGDEN. *(composing himself)* I feel like I'm being interrogated.

INTERVIEWER. . . . . .

DR OGDEN. Well, yes, anyway, we named her Frisky, but she's been anything but. We were hopeful that it would act as an omen, you know? But it's not just her fault. I mean, the males are as much to blame. To be frank. Actually the last but one male panda we had here was called Frank. *(does not even crack a smile)* Funny. Yes, I think we were just getting a little tired of the whole Ling Ling, Chi Chi, Xin Xin naming kind of thing and wanted to shake things up a bit, but old Frank just took one look at Frisky here and turned his back to her immediately. "Not if she was the last female panda on earth", which of course she very nearly was at the time and now is. But no, Frank wasn't having any of it. "No way, Jose". Oh, he had a number of health issues and when we finally did get him fighting fit, he died, so... *(A beat)* Yes, but despite the setbacks, my team and I have always made sure that we maintained high spirits about the place. Morale has always been good here. No one around here can be accused of being glum. *Au contraire* there's been plenty of shits and giggles, plenty of *joie de vivre.* I've started using French expressions. I love foreign languages. I wish I could speak one. I had a translator once, he was from Norway and he could speak seven. He was a close friend but he died of a broken heart or pancreatic cancer or some such thing. My translators since haven't really been up to much. He's been a hard act to follow really...

INTERVIEWER. . . . . .

FRISKY. You're avoiding the issue.

DR OGDEN. What?

FRISKY. You are.

DR OGDEN. I'm not.

FRISKY. You are. *(A beat)* Tell her about Max.

DR OGDEN. Max?

FRISKY. Max.

DR OGDEN. *(to* **INTERVIEWER***)* Max was the last male panda...

FRISKY. Well, he needn't have been.

DR OGDEN. *(snapping a little)* Will you let me tell the story, please?

(**FRISKY** *goes back to chewing on her bamboo.*)

INTERVIEWER. . . . . . .

(pause)

DR OGDEN. The thing is...well, after Frank. And even before really...well, Frisky's been here for the longest time, haven't you, girl? And well, we got kind of close, didn't we? You'd admit that?

(**FRISKY** *continues nonchalantly chewing on bamboo.*)

Nothing untoward, you understand. Nothing disgusting. Just, when you work alongside someone, with someone, you get, well you get kind of fond of each other. In a way. What with the media events, the photo opportunities, the travelling together, or just here at the enclosure. You bond. Like I said, nothing untoward, nothing disgusting, but I just had these... well, thoughts.

(**FRISKY** *stops chewing on bamboo.*)

Nothing sexual...

(**FRISKY** *continues chewing on bamboo.*)

But just something deeper, you know? Like a connection that transcended everything I'd known before. It was, well, beautiful. It was safe. And I started to see her chastity as a kind of faithfulness to me. Like a form of monogamy, kind of thing. I was very touched by it. Then Frank joined us and well, like I say, he just didn't fancy it, or her, and he passed away. And then it was just me and Frisky again. It was like old times... that was, well, until we got the call from Vienna...

FRISKY. That was about Max probably.

DR OGDEN. Yes.

INTERVIEWER. . . . . .

DR OGDEN. They had someone there. Well, a panda. Called Max. They said he had fucked their last female to death over there. Literally. But they were confident that Frisky was made of stronger stuff and could they send him over, because they were closing anyway. We said *(with some regret)* "sure"...

INTERVIEWER. . . . . .

DR OGDEN. Meantime, while the Austrians were working on all the red tape, the remaining pandas in Asia, Australia, North America, here in Europe, well, the pandas, they were dropping like flies and no one knew why, but we all agreed to keep it quiet for the time being. It became obvious to me that it was down to us here in London to keep the whole panda show going, as it were. We were down to just Max and Frisky. Well I felt torn. I felt nauseous. *(A beat)* So the day arrives and they bring him out and my team took one look at him and they just knew right away. I mean they were high-fiving each other. It was like a space launch. Max, well he just exuded something, you see. It was like you could bet your house on him. And he was...well...let's just say, he was attractive...

(**DR OGDEN** *pours himself a glass of water and downs it.*)

I told my team to take the afternoon off. That I'd handle it from here. I think they went bowling. I led Max through that tunnel on your way in here and I just couldn't stop thinking about him having his paws all over Frisky. It made me sick to my stomach. He bounded into the enclosure like he owned the place and well, they both lit up when they saw each other. It was instant, you know. Almost electric or magnetic. Frisky never once looked at me like she looked at Max that day. *(A beat)* Anyway, I just couldn't take it, so I picked up that rifle over there and I shot him.

(silence)

That shocks you, I expect.

INTERVIEWER. . . . . .

DR OGDEN. It was a crime of passion really. But I know that doesn't make it alright.

(longer silence)

My translator was from Denmark not Norway...and he drowned. He was...a good man. *(A beat)* There's a part of me, and I hate this part of me, that's just hell bent on the pursuit. To advance, you know? I'd like to love. I love the concept. I want to love freely but I just can't let things bloom. I can't let it come to me or just occur because what if it won't? I'm insecure. If it's not something to chase, to get, or to control, I'm just not sure I recognize its worth. I just end up destroying things. I'm selfish. *(a beat)* My arm still hurts from that gate coming in. *(a beat)* I don't know, I'm just human, I guess.

INTERVIEWER. *(shaking her electronic device that no longer works)* . . . . .

FRISKY. *(with an orgasmic build)* The sky over Genoa is orange and black. The clouds are purple and green. All in all it's a screaming mess. It's spreading everywhere now. The wind is screeching, birds are flying into each other, planes are falling out of the sky. Everyone's yelling but no one ever listens. The ocean's had enough, it's no longer just a spray, crashing its waves over the tall buildings you built, puking up its underworld all over you all. It's a great spectacle. It's no longer a secret. It's freezing. Everyone's drowning. No souvenir photograph, no dog collar jingle, no translators to help, nothing works now. Any money that anyone ever made, all the conversations in bed anyone ever had, all those laughs, all those whispers, all those promises and kisses, gone, once were, not now, forgotten. It had to stop here. You knew it was coming, you could have done more...That's it really... *(She drops dead.)*

INTERVIEWER. . . . . . .

DR OGDEN. Gosh.

(blackout)

End of Play

Old Flame

Mira Gibson

OLD FLAME was produced as part of the 38th Annual Samuel French Off Off Broadway Short Play Festival at the Clurman Theater at Theater Row in New York City on July 24, 2013. It was directed by Mira Gibson. The cast was as follows:

HANNAH. . . . . Keira Keeley

JACK . . . . .Sam Breslin Wright

SOPHIA. . . . . Andrea Syglowski

HENRY . . . . Robert Askins

CHARACTERS

HANNAH – trying to see the silver lining (mid 30s)
JACK – the old flame (mid 30s)
SOPHIA – the old flame's girlfriend (mid 20s)
HENRY – Hannah's boyfriend (early 40s)

SETTING

A grocery store somewhere.

ABOUT THE PLAYWRIGHT

A playwright, screenwriter, and director, Mira Gibson is a recent alum of Youngblood, the writers group at Ensemble Studio Theatre. Mira's plays have been produced at Rattlestick's Theaterjam (*Old Flame*, 2013), Williamstown Theater Festival (*Nico*, 2009), Ensemble Studio Theater (*Master of None* and *The Red White and Blue Process*, 2009), Eclectic Company Theater of Los Angeles (*Master of None*, 2009), The 52nd Street Project (*Midnight in the Alley of One Dream*), and the Midtown International Theater Festival (*Childhood Montana*, 2008); further plays have received developmental readings at Rattlestick Playwrights Theater, Southampton Playwriting Conference, Long Beach Playhouse, and the Youngblood Bloodworks Reading Series. Her one-act play *The Red White and Blue Process* received a commission from The Sloan Foundation. In 2012 Mira's first screenplay, Warfield was produced by Summer Smoke Productions, starred her twin sister, and screened at modest film festivals around NYC.

(Sunday, late morning. A grocery store, mostly empty.)

(HANNAH consults a handwritten grocery list, then places some spices into her basket. She thumbs through a rumpled stack of coupons to see whether or not she might get a deal on the spices.)

(JACK enters the other end of the aisle. He carelessly tosses items into his basket not really paying attention to what he's grabbing. He has a bit of a double take when he sees HANNAH.)

JACK. Don't forget to make sure Mrs. Dash is on sale.

HANNAH. I'm way ahead of you.

JACK. You haven't changed a bit.

HANNAH. *(finally looks at who's talking to her)* Oh my God. Hey.

JACK. You look just the same.

HANNAH. It hasn't been that long.

JACK. It kind of has.

HANNAH. Has it?

JACK. It has for me.

HANNAH. Why was it so "long" for you?

JACK. I don't know. Life, you know? Takes forever to get where you want to be, but goes by so fast.

HANNAH. Yeah. Where do you want to be?

JACK. I think I'm there.

HANNAH. Really?

JACK. Does the ramen, condoms, and pasta sauce not give it away?

HANNAH. Ah. It does. Should've known.

JACK. But I guess, it's just, you get to a certain place in life and figure, this is it.

HANNAH. I can't believe you're saying that because that's completely what I've been thinking recently.

JACK. In a good way?

HANNAH. Yeah, in a good way.

JACK. Because for me it's totally in a good way.

HANNAH. Me too, it sounds like I'm settling, but I'm not, I'm good.

JACK. Good, me too.

HANNAH. Great.

JACK. I'm so glad you're doing well.

HANNAH. Yeah I'm doing real well.

JACK. Because when we were breaking up, I thought, I don't know, I thought maybe I broke you or something.

HANNAH. My heart?

JACK. Yeah, or, all of you.

HANNAH. You did.

(beat)

When did you move back?

JACK. Six months ago.

HANNAH. How was L.A.?

JACK. I gave it a shot.

HANNAH. It went well?

JACK. I made a killing selling used cars. Then I got used to it and decided I wanted something new and different.

HANNAH. You've always been so free like that. Like a rolling stone, I guess.

JACK. Hannah, are you ok?

HANNAH. I don't care and I'm fine, and I don't mean to sound like I care at all, but we kind of always talked as though you'd let me know when you came back, like we were only breaking up because you were leaving.

JACK. That was why we had to break up.

HANNAH. So… you tell me.

JACK. Things change. Don't they?

(beat)

Oh look. Mop slippers. So you can mop while you walk around the apartment.

HANNAH. I already have those.

JACK. So where do you live nowadays?

HANNAH. Same place.

JACK. So far away from everyone still?

HANNAH. It's ok, I have cats now.

JACK. You're way too hot to be a cat lady.

HANNAH. *(shrugs)* I've finally given in to it.

JACK. Well I hope at the very least you're still a slut.

HANNAH. Not really, Jack.

JACK. *(grabs his heart as though it was just pierced)* Men across New York City weep!

HANNAH. You always gave the strangest compliments.

JACK. Jumping into bed on the first date: Man, that's when I fell in love with you. It was non-stop passion; that's how I remember us. I didn't know how rare it was. Remember how we used to speak in code? No matter what we were talking about, if someone joined us and we wanted to keep our conversation going we could speak in metaphors and symbolism until the new guy felt awkward and walked away. We were the best at parties.

HANNAH. You're an idiot. *(waits for a response)* You're a real son-of a-bitch. I never got to say that to you because you completely cut me off after you moved, but that's what I think you are. A real bastard.

JACK. It was fun being with you, I'm not trying to offend you.

HANNAH. It was fun. It was great. It was like floating through a dream. That's how it was for me. It was great. I got used to it. I depended on it. And when you left it was really shitty for a really really long time.

JACK. I'm sorry.

HANNAH. Don't be sorry. It was better. It was better than being with you, because feeling that shitty was as alive as I've ever felt. I don't expect you to get that, but that's what's really going on with me, not that I'd ever let anyone know.

JACK. So you still feel that way? Shitty?

HANNAH. Yeah, but I stuff it pretty far down and ignore it most of the time.

JACK. Something I haven't told anyone, and maybe didn't even know until now: I've missed you.

HANNAH. Is that a real statement?

JACK. Yes, it's a real statement.

HANNAH. You don't know who I am now, how I face the world, you don't know me like you think you do.

JACK. I'm catching on, Hannah. And believe me when I say, I feel I've missed you.

HANNAH. Really?

(**SOPHIA** *glides down the aisle, pleased to have finally found her beau.*)

SOPHIA. There you are! Why was I wasting my time in the beer aisle? (*to* **HANNAH**) Hi! Thanks for finding him!

JACK. This is my girlfriend, Sophia.

HANNAH. I'm Hannah.

SOPHIA. This is Hannah.? I've heard so much about you. (*gravely*) How are you?

HANNAH. Remember Sisyphus? And how he was condemned to roll a boulder up a hill over and over again for all of eternity? The only way he could be free is if he chooses to roll the boulder up the hill. So every single time he's at the bottom of the hill he says to himself "I choose this"; he hates it, but he chooses it, and therefore he's free.

(**SOPHIA** *totally doesn't get it and laughs awkwardly.*)

SOPHIA. She's so quirky!

JACK. Hannah was just telling me how she still lives in our old place.

HANNAH. *(to* **SOPHIA***)* Yes, same apartment for the past eight years, I guess I'm loyal. How long have you lived in the city?

SOPHIA. Oh gosh, how long's it been, Jack? We moved here together.

HANNAH. You did?

SOPHIA. Yeah we were living it up in L.A. and when Jack wanted to move back, we both thought, why end a good thing? Right, babe?

JACK. That's more or less the story.

SOPHIA. *(faux whispers to* **HANNAH***)* More the story!

JACK. *(for real whispers to* **HANNAH***)* Less.

(Subtly, like the waft of a subway fart, **HENRY** *appears holding up a can of cat food.)*

HENRY. Is this the right stuff? Shredded turkey in gravy wet cat food? Friskies?

(to **JACK***)* This is Henry, he knows my brand.

(Why does this small victory feel like a defeat?)

HANNAH. *(to* **HENRY***)* Yeah, babe, that's what we want.

HENRY. Should we load up? Do the usual thirty cans?

HANNAH. Shh- give it here.

*(***HANNAH** *snatches the can and throws it into her basket.)*

SOPHIA. How many cats do you have?

HANNAH.	**HENRY.**
Two.	Six.

JACK. Jesus.

HENRY. Hannah had two, and I had one. And Hannah's were tormenting mine, so we got Charlie to ease the tension, but we didn't neuter him in time, and Hannah thought Kitty was spayed, but she wasn't. And neither of us has the heart to give any of them away. So. You know. It's been a real nightmare.

HANNAH. Henry, this is Jack, an old boyfriend of mine, and Sophia.

HENRY. Hi!

JACK. Should I be worried Hannah's told you all about me?

HENRY. *(blank stare)* No. I haven't really heard a thing. I don't think Hannah's ever told me about any of her old flames.

JACK. *(surprisingly disappointed)* Well... that's a relief...

SOPHIA. We should probably get going, babe, we don't want to be late for the barbeque.

HENRY. Oh, is it a mother's day barbeque?

SOPHIA. A what?

HANNAH. It's mother's day. Henry and I are picking up a few things, we're going to go out to the Island and cook my mom dinner.

JACK. That's so good of you.

HANNAH. Good of me? Good of Henry!

(**HANNAH** *and* **HENRY** *share a laugh.*)

HENRY. I know! The cats and the mother! Guess I like this one!

(They all have a good laugh.)

HANNAH. It's not that bad!

(They laugh more.)

HENRY. It kind of is.

(The laughter dies down.)

HANNAH. Well I think we have everything.

HENRY. Here. I can get this rung up.

(He takes **HANNAH**'*s shopping basket.*)

Oops, almost forgot! Can I have the coupons?

HANNAH. Good thinking!

(**HANNAH** *hands* **HENRY** *the crumpled coupons.*)

HENRY. My bets in for $3.99.

HANNAH. No way, six dollars at least.

HENRY. Really? Record!

HANNAH. Record!

JACK. What's that?

HANNAH. We place bets on how much we'll save with our coupons.

HENRY. See you down there? Nice meeting you both.

(HENRY *exits.*)

(JACK *hands his basket to* SOPHIA.)

JACK. I'll meet you in the beer aisle.

SOPHIA. Ah, ok! It was nice meeting you!

HANNAH. You too.

(*It's hard to get back into a real conversation, but eventually:*)

JACK. You seem happy to me.

HANNAH. Maybe I am. I can't tell anymore.

JACK. Ask me if I'm happy.

HANNAH. I don't think I want to know.

JACK. Could we get coffee sometime?

(*A pregnant pause while* HANNAH *considers this. Then:*)

(*blackout*)

End of Play

Reality Play

Mark Swaner

REALITY PLAY was produced as part of the 38th Annual Samuel French Off Off Broadway Short Play Festival at the Clurman Theater at Theater Row in New York City on July 26, 2013. The cast was as follows:

ACTOR . . . . Mark Swaner

ACTOR . . . . Parvesh Cheena

CHARACTERS

ACTOR
ACTRESS

Both characters can be played by actors of any gender.

ABOUT THE PLAYWRIGHT

Mark Swaner studied playwriting as an undergraduate the University of Iowa. After school he spent five years working at The Second City in Chicago, performing in the mainstage hit, Between Barak and a Hard Place. Mark's plays have been seen in City Theatre's Summer Shorts and the 24 Hour Theater Project in Miami and he premiered his one-man-show, *I Miss Racism* in Los Angeles. Most recently Swaner has been writing for NBC working with Late Night with Jimmy Fallon. While working in Chicago, Mark appeared on the reality show Top Chef. You can follow him on Twitter @mswaner.

Mark Swaner is currently shopping a pilot about life aboard a cruise ship and a Hollywood action comedy called *Above the Title.* He is seeking excellent representation

(The lights are full work lights and the stage is set by stagehands in full view. It is as if you are in a studio watching a TV taping. On a cart, there is an overhead projector, a stack of overhead transparencies, a bottle of rum, a small beaker with warm water, a jar of mayonnaise, a spoon and a cell phone. There is also a powerful vacuum and small keyboard. We hear the real audio of the cues being prepared in the booth. **ACTOR** *and* **ACTRESS** *casually walk out to their positions.)*

STAGE MANAGER (O.S.). Cue 61 stand by...61 go.

(Lights down. The overhead stays up and reads "This is a Reality Play. Please turn your phones on to enable voting." Lights up on **ACTOR**. **ACTRESS** *changes the transparency to one that reads* **"REALITY PLAY".)**

ACTOR. Reality TV provided me the single most transformative thing I ever saw on television. The show was called "Man Versus Beast" and it pit people against animals in different kinds of competitions. It was magnificent. The highlight was a hotdog eating contest between humanities' champion – that Japanese guy who wins all those hotdog eating contests – and a Kodiak Bear.

*(***ACTRESS*** changes the transparency to one that has a picture of Takeru Kobayashi eating hot dogs and a picture of a Kodiak bear.)*

ACTOR. 8 minutes of a 2000lb bear that doesn't know it's in a contest and a terrified Japanese man pounding hot dogs. I knew then that a cultural paradigm shift was occurring. It was at that moment...

*(***ACTRESS*** changes the transparency to one that has a picture of 40 harnessed little people pulling an airplane.)*

ACTOR. *(cont.)* (or maybe when 40 dwarves pulled an airplane faster than an elephant) that "reality" conquered absurdism and took it from the rest of the arts. Sorry Dali. Some say that this marks the downfall of our civilization. And it is true that during their fall, Roman citizens crowded the colosseum to watch a Christian lose an eating contest with a bear. But even if we know better, these shows remain incredibly compelling to us. So I will endeavor an experiment. I will attempt to combine the essential elements of a reality show into a live theater event. To see if it, too, will be compelling. I will be assisted in my experiment by (*insert* **ACTRESS'** *real name*). Now I have identified five essential elements of a reality show. The first...

(**ACTRESS** *reveals the next transparency. It reads* **"PHYSICAL HUMILIATION"** *and has pictures of contestants on "The Biggest Loser" and "Wipeout" being humiliated.* **ACTOR** *takes his shirt off.*)

ACTOR. *(cont.)* ...is physical humiliation. Reality shows use physical humiliation to provide the audience schadenfreude, taking enjoyment in the suffering of others. To simulate this, I will allow (*insert* **ACTRESS'** *real name*) to apply this (*insert brand name*) vacuum to my exposed body.

(**ACTRESS** *has rolled the vacuum next to* **ACTOR**. *She turns it on and begins sucking the fat on* **ACTOR**'s *chest with the hose attachment. She keeps applying the vacuum until she needs to change a transparency or some other business, at which time she sticks the running vacuum to* **ACTOR**'s *gut and moves to her next step. When able, she should return to vacuum.*)

ACTOR. Now in order to cope with the rigors of Element 1, a codependent element is needed. And that is Element B. Booze.

(**ACTRESS** *changes the transparency to one reading* **"BOOZE"** *with pictures from drunks on "Jersey Shore" and "Real Housewives".* **ACTRESS** *hands actor a pint bottle of booze, which* **ACTOR** *opens and chugs. He drinks repeatedly throughout the next portion.*)

ACTOR. It is everywhere, the grease that makes the engine hum. Now anyone that says this isn't enough booze for a proper experiment should know that I was already pretty loaded when I got here. That brings us to the third element. I call this "Dietary Distress."

(ACTRESS *changes the transparency and it reads* "EATING SHIT".)

ACTOR. From having to eat horse semen on "Fear Factor" to NBA semen on "The Kardashians", reality stars suffer dietary distress. To simulate this, I will drink this beaker of warm water mixed with a dollop of mayonnaise.

(ACTRESS *mixes the water and mayonnaise and* ACTOR *drinks it. He comes close to vomiting. He swigs some booze to wash it down.*)

ACTOR. Physical Humiliation, dietary distress and booze when combined very often produces emotional humiliation. Often in the form of a confessional.

(ACTRESS *changes the transparency and it reads* "EMOTIONAL HUMILIATION" *and has pictures of people sobbing. She turns off the vacuum.* ACTOR *faces out and steps into a special.*)

ACTOR. I am a strong person, but I'm not the strongest person. I know I didn't come here to make friends, I came to win.

(ACTRESS *puts up a transparency that reads* "MANIPULATIVE MUSIC". *She then plays emotional music on the keyboard underneath* ACTOR*'s speech.*)

ACTOR. My Dad has always been my hero and now that he's battling cancer I want him to know...FUCK!!! GODDAMNIT! ENOUGH! I'm trying to do the only honest part of this whole show and you're still fucking just over there doing your shit. Fuck it! The moment is ruined now! Let's just get this over with. What's next?

(**ACTRESS** *puts up a transparency that reads* ***"INAPPROPRIATE FITS OF ANGER"*** *with pictures of screaming. A beat.*)

ACTOR. Right covered that. Next.

(**ACTRESS** *changes the transparency it reads* ***"MAKE-OVER!!!"*** *Up-beat music plays and lights move. The* **ACTRESS** *instantly redresses the* **ACTOR** *in a onepiece suit, shirt and tie. She fixes his hair and face to look amazing. The music and lights stop only moments after they began.*)

ACTOR. I feel like a whole new person. What's next?

ACTRESS *changes the transparency. It reads:*

(*"Voting and Elimination: Text your vote to (***)-***-****. For (insert* **ACTOR***'s real name) text the number 1 to the number above. For (insert* **ACTRESS***'s real name) text the number 2. For (insert another actor's real name) text the number 3. For (insert another actor's real name) text the number 4. For (insert another actor's real name) text the number 5. Normal fees for texting and data apply".*)

ACTOR. This brings us to the final element to complete our reality play. Voting and elimination. Only one of us can be the subject of this experiment and it is up to you the audience to decide who it will be. Will I continue and do this play in tomorrow night's show or will I be replaced by another actor from the cast? To vote for me, text the number 1 to (***)-***-****.

ACTRESS. And to vote for me, text the number 2 to (***)-***-****.

PERSON 3. And to vote for me, text the number 3 to (***)-***-****.

PERSON 4. And to vote for me, text the number 4 to (***)-***-****.

PERSON 5. And to vote for me, text the number 5 to (***)-***-****.

ACTOR. You have 30 seconds to vote starting...right now.

(The cast holds hands and the lights move very dramatically and music is heard. They smile and hug. Or scowl at each other.)

ACTOR. The actor that will be moving on and playing this role in Reality Play will be...the actor will be...the actor will be...revealed tomorrow night.

(Blackout, only the overhead projector is left. The last transparency reads:)

"REALITY PLAY. Created by Mark Swaner. Voting outcomes may be altered by the producers in consultation with Actor's Equity Association and the (insert the name of the theater)."

End of Play.

Tattoo You

Lisa Kenner Grissom

TATTOO YOU was produced as part of the 38th Annual Samuel French Off Off Broadway Short Play Festival at the Clurman Theater at Theater Row in New York City on July 24, 2013. It was directed by Brandt Reiter. The cast was as follows:

TAMMY . . . . Carrie Ann Quinn

RACHEL . . . . Elizabeth Dement

CHARACTERS

TAMMY – (late 30s) wears skinny jeans that are too tight and a low cut shirt. Trying to look younger than she can pull off. Tammy has no sense of boundaries.

RACHEL – (late 30s) is polished in a skirt and top, accessorized with a designer scarf and interesting jewelry. Age-appropriate. Rachel is polite to a fault.

SETTING

A girls' bathroom in a suburban public high school on the occasion of a 20th reunion gathering. This particular bathroom is one of the smaller ones in the school. You'd need to know where it is.

TIME

Late afternoon approaching evening.
The present.

PLAYWRIGHT'S NOTES

The high school depicted is located in one of Boston's many suburbs, with a mixed population of working, middle and upper class families.

However, this high school could be located in a similar suburb of another city. References to Boston, the Museum of Fine Arts, et cetera can be interchanged for another city with similar characteristics and locales.

PRODUCTION NOTES

/ A slash indicates overlapping or simultaneous dialogue. The number of slashes from line to line indicate a quickening of pace.

– A dash indicates interrupted dialogue.

The actors face the audience, as if the bathroom mirrors are hanging along the fourth wall.

PROPS

Rachel: An expensive handbag. Two expensive lipsticks. Designer scarf.
Tammy: A cheap knock-off handbag. Drugstore makeup. A cell phone.

ABOUT THE PLAYWRIGHT

Lisa Kenner Grissom's play *Tattoo You* (National 10-Minute Play Award winner, The Kennedy Center American College Theater Festival) has been seen by audiences in Washington D.C., Boston, New York and Los Angeles. Other short plays include: *the girls* (Boston Theatre Marathon), *Orangutan & Lulu* (Estrogenius Festival), *Drinks Before Flight* (Boston Theatre Marathon). Full-length plays include: *MOTHERLAND* (semi-finalist: Princess Grace Playwriting Fellowship), *Chambers* (finalist: O'Neill National Playwrights Conference, The Lark, WordBRIDGE). Lisa attended the O'Neill Playwrights Conference as a Kennedy Center Fellow and Playwright Observer and was a finalist for the Playwrights' Center Core Apprentice Program. Her work has been presented and/or developed at The Kennedy Center, Boston Playwrights' Theatre, The Clurman Theater, Manhattan Theatre Source, The Blank Theatre, The Road Theatre Company, Theatre of NOTE, and others. B.A. Wesleyan University; MFA Lesley University. Lisa is a proud member of The Dramatist Guild and The Playwrights Union. www.lisakennergrissom.com

(A suburban public high school bathroom. The bathroom is rather typical with a couple of stalls, two sinks, and a mirror above each sink.)

(RACHEL is polished in a skirt and top, accessorized with a designer scarf and interesting jewelry. Age-appropriate. RACHEL's defining characteristic is her hair.)

(RACHEL enters the bathroom. She looks to see if anyone is inside. She is alone and relieved of that fact. She takes a few palpable moments to study the space, taking it in. She looks at the wall, maybe notices some graffiti. Peeks into the stalls. Then, in front of the sink farthest from the door, she looks at her reflection in the mirror. Smooths her hair.)

(TAMMY enters. She wears skinny jeans that are too tight and a low cut shirt. Trying to look younger than she can pull off. They look like they are from completely different worlds.)

(RACHEL sees TAMMY's reflection in the mirror. Their eyes meet. A suspended moment. Then,)

TAMMY. Rachel Slater? Is that you?

RACHEL. Hi! – I'm sorry, I don't remember names/so well

TAMMY. I saw someone in the hall and I thought/that was you

RACHEL. This is really strange –

TAMMY. Oh My God. Rachel Slater!

RACHEL. There will be name tags, right? They always have name tags at these things –

TAMMY. It's me – Tammy Donlon.

(TAMMY gives RACHEL a major hug, catching her by surprise. RACHEL doesn't hug back.)

RACHEL. Oh! I'm early. I just came in here to/you know

(**RACHEL** *takes an expensive lipstick from her handbag and applies it.* **TAMMY** *checks her out.*)

TAMMY. That's pretty. *(beat)* Can I see what color?

RACHEL. Uh. Sure.

(**TAMMY** *plucks the lipstick from* **RACHEL**. *She moves in front of the sink/mirror closest to the door and applies the lipstick. She talks to* **RACHEL** *through her reflection in the mirror.*)

TAMMY. You look amazing, Rachel. Really amazing.

(**TAMMY** *takes drugstore makeup items from her handbag and primps.*)

RACHEL. Oh. You too. Your hair is so dark now. You used to have that *(blonde)* –

TAMMY. I know, I know. It just...turned brown one day.

(**TAMMY** *fusses with her hair. Gives up.*)

RACHEL. That was a big part of your look back then.

TAMMY. Your hair was so long and shiny. I mean, it still is –

RACHEL. It's a little less...big, I guess you'd say.

TAMMY. The big hair!! It was so...*(she makes a descriptive gesture)*...remember?

(**RACHEL** *nods and smiles halfheartedly.*)

Mine's flat now. Yours is so full.

(**RACHEL** *fiddles with her hair.*)

RACHEL. Thanks. Well, I'll see you out there –

(**TAMMY**, *in between* **RACHEL** *and the door, starts to dance.*)

TAMMY. Hey – hang on a sec! I wonder who's gonna be here tonight. Remember the bands? They were always kinda lame but the dances...I always loved the dances...

(**TAMMY** *continues dancing and tries to encourage* **RACHEL** *to join in, but* **RACHEL** *doesn't.*)

Didn't you?

RACHEL. Yeah, sure.

(*TAMMY stops dancing.*)

TAMMY. I still live in town, y'know. Three generations of Donlons. No one's going anywhere. Married a firefighter – do you remember Quinn Sutton? Quinnie? Football team?

(*RACHEL returns to primping.*)

RACHEL. Of course.

TAMMY. You wrote that article on him for the school paper with a picture and every/thing

RACHEL. You have a good memory. I don't really remem/ber

TAMMY. I think he always liked you a little.

RACHEL. We just sat near each other from grade school on... you know, Slater and Sutton. *(beat)* What does he look like now?

(*TAMMY returns to her makeup. She still has RACHEL's lipstick.*)

TAMMY. He's still hot if that's what you/mean!

RACHEL. I didn't – no – I was just wondering...

TAMMY. We hooked up summer after senior year and that was it. What about you?

RACHEL. I got married after grad school.

TAMMY. Oh. Some are working on their second marriage, so maybe you had the right idea to wait. Y'know what? You kinda lost your accent!

RACHEL. Right...sometimes these things/fade

TAMMY. It can come back though 'cause it's in your DNA. I wanna hear it! I'll help you bring it back! It'll be a riot –

(*TAMMY laughs at her idea. RACHEL tries to laugh it off.*)

RACHEL. I don't think so. I'm gonna see if they need me to put out decorations or –

(It's subtle but **TAMMY** *does not create space for* **RACHEL** *to get by.)*

TAMMY. Wait – you moved away, right? I mean, I know you did because otherwise I'd have seen you around.

*(***TAMMY*** laughs at herself.)*

RACHEL. I live in Chicago. I'm a curator of antiquities.

TAMMY. What does that mean?

RACHEL. I have my masters in art history and I work with ancient artifacts from all over the world and put together large-scale art exhibitions. I'm sure you've been to the Museum of Fine Arts downtown?

TAMMY. You mean Boston?

RACHEL. Yes. You must have been to the museum? It's one of the/best.

TAMMY. Not so much. Actually, never. I stay close to home.

RACHEL. Right. This town seems the same.

TAMMY. Yeah it pretty much is. Things change here and there...people, y'know. You got kids? I got three.

RACHEL. I have one. He's four.

TAMMY. I had mine right outta school.

RACHEL. Where'd you go?

TAMMY. What do you mean?

RACHEL. Oh. Sorry. Right.

TAMMY. Yeah I got pregnant and then stayed home with the kids. The oldest is nineteen/

RACHEL. Wow/

TAMMY. Then fifteen and thirteen. See this?

*(***TAMMY*** lifts up her shirt and moves toward* **RACHEL** *to show her a scar where she had a caesarian.* **RACHEL** *looks at it curiously.)*

RACHEL. Is that a tattoo? Of the scar? –

(There is a tattoo over the scar, actually of the scar itself – making a section of the stitches appear permanent.

TAMMY *rubs it unconsciously, then pulls her shirt back down. This all happens quickly.)*

TAMMY. Yeah/

RACHEL. Huh/

TAMMY. Scars fade but tattoos are permanent. My kids... they made me grow up. I did it to remember that. Do you have any?

RACHEL. Like I said, I have a little boy.

TAMMY. I mean tattoos.

RACHEL. No...that's not my thing.

*(**RACHEL** fusses with her scarf. Tries one way. Then another.)*

TAMMY. Everyone has scars though. Wanna touch it?

*(**TAMMY** moves toward her.)*

RACHEL. No thanks.

TAMMY. I'm just kidding!! I'm just messing with you. You should have seen your/face

*(Throughout this section, **TAMMY** subtly blocks **RACHEL** from the door. **RACHEL** tries to stay polite as she navigates this.)*

RACHEL. Yeah...I'm gonna head in –

*(**TAMMY** finds a photo on her phone and puts it in front of **RACHEL**.)*

TAMMY. Hey! Look at this picture of my kids.

RACHEL. Huh...I can see/Quinn

*(**TAMMY** scrolls through a few more photos, showing them to **RACHEL**.)*

TAMMY. They get into a lot of trouble. Like me. Not like you. You were a good kid.

RACHEL. We didn't know each other that well/really

TAMMY. One of them in particular. My girl. She went through a lot. With the other girls. Y'know –

*(Agitated, **RACHEL** continues fussing with her scarf.)*

RACHEL. People will be arriving soon, so I'll just see you out there –

TAMMY. So my girl she had a…situation and it made me remember all this stuff –

RACHEL. It's in the gym, right?/

TAMMY. What I'm trying to say is – I'm sorry for all those things –

RACHEL. I don't know what you're talking about.

TAMMY. This is the bathroom.

(The briefest of moments, suspended.)

RACHEL. I'll see you out there, Tammy.

(RACHEL tries to move past TAMMY who is in between her and the door. TAMMY doesn't move.)

TAMMY. Rachel, just listen to me for a sec –

RACHEL. Listen to me Tammy. I came here to have a drink or two, match a few faces with some name tags and see the people who meant something to me at this place. I didn't come to hear your confession in the bathroom.

TAMMY. My daughter came home one day. Her clothes all ripped and torn and I asked her what happened and she said she fell. But she didn't fall. Those rips weren't from a fall. Because I know those rips. I know what it takes to make them. And I told her, I said –

(RACHEL gets right in TAMMY's face. It's as violent a gesture as it can be without touching. TAMMY is genuinely frightened.)

RACHEL. Tammy. I want you to shut your lip glossed mouth. I want you to live in whatever private hell you live in where you try to "teach" your daughter things you never learned. You can try to erase what you did, but you can't. It's permanent. *(beat)* Just like your tattoo.

(The moment hangs in the air. Then, TAMMY moves away from the door. RACHEL collects herself in front of the mirror. Smooths her skirt, her hair. Takes a breath.)

(Realizing she still has **RACHEL**'s *lipstick,* **TAMMY** *tries to hand it back. She holds it out but* **RACHEL** *doesn't take it.)*

(Instead, **RACHEL** *takes another expensive lipstick from her handbag. She re-applies, moving her lips back and forth. She smiles in the mirror.)*

Will Quinn be here tonight?

TAMMY. Uh...yeah.

RACHEL. I can't wait to see him. He sat behind me all through school. *(beat)* He used to play with my hair. *(beat)* I always liked that.

*(***RACHEL** *fluffs her hair and exits. The door slams behind her.)*

*(***TAMMY** *stands alone in front of the mirror. A moment passes before she slowly wipes the lip gloss from her mouth.)*

(lights out)

End of Play

Tornado

Arlitia Jones

TORNADO was produced by Blue Roses Productions as part of the 38th Annual Samuel French Off Off Broadway Short Play Festival at the Clurman Theater at Theater Row in New York City on July 25th, 2013. It was directed by Erma Duricko. Original music was created for the production by Tim Brown The cast was as follows:

SHAUN LOCKER............................George R. Sheffey
JASON ....Dominic Comperatore

CHARACTERS

SHAUN LOCKER – 43, a large heavy-set man, tall, professional looking
JASON – late 30s, owner small store that sells sports uniforms

SETTING

The play opens in the interior of Jason's sporting goods store in Seattle, Washington. Jason is working at the counter. Shaun is wandering among the racks, sort of lost. He stops and stares at a wall of uniforms. He's wearing a casual suit. His overall appearance is slightly disheveled. Jason watches him for a few moments before he speaks.

ABOUT THE PLAYWRIGHT

Arlitia Jones is a playwright and poet, as well as co-founder of TossPot Productions in Anchorage, Alaska. She is a member of Seattle Repertory Theatre's Playwrights Writing Group. Her lastest full-length play *Summerland*, based on the true story of Spirit Photographer William Mumler has been selected for Seattle Repertory Theatre's 2014 New Play Festival. She is also currently at work adapting *A Christmas Carol* along with Director Michael Haney for Perseverance Theatre's 2014 Anchorage season. Her play *Come to me, Leopards*, had a workshop production in October 2013 at Cyrano's Theatre in Anchorage. Her play *Rush at Everlasting* received a reading with the Northwest Playwrights' Alliance at the Seattle Repertory Theatre in Spring 2012 at The Lark in New York City in 2013 and a world premiere production at Perseverance Theatre in Juneau, Alaska in January 2014, and Anchorage in February 2014. In addition to being selected for the 38th Annual Samuel French OOB Short Play Festival last year, her short play *Tornado* was also selected as the National Award Winner in the 2014 Summer Shorts Festival with City Theatre in Miami, FL. She is the recipient of an Individual Artists Fellowship from the Rasmuson Foundation. She is a recent writing residency alumna at Hedgebrook and will be an upcoming writer in residence at Djerassi Resident Artists Program in Fall 2014 where she will be working on her latest play *The Ugly Children of Eve: A Fairytale for Labor* about Mother Jones and the Colorado Coal Strikes. Jones traveled to New York City in July 2013 to participate as an emerging playwright in the 2013 Director's Lab at Lincoln Center. Past works include *The Emperical Eskimo* which was selected as a finalist in the 2011 36th Annual Samuel French OOB Summer Play Festival. *Make Good the Fires*, commissioned by the Alaska Humanities Forum and Cyrano's was produced in 2009 in Anchorage. *Sway Me Moon* produced by Three Wise Moose at Out North Theatre in February of 2008 in Anchorage and again at the 2008 Last Frontier Theatre Conference. Her short plays have been staged in Anchorage's Overnighter Theatre. With TossPot Productions, Jones directed Arthur Jolly's *A Gulag Mouse*, in Anchorage in March 2013. In addition to her theatre work, Jones is also a published poet and author of one volume, *The Bandsaw Riots* which won the 2001 Dorothy Brunsman Prize from Bear Star Press. Her poems have appeared in numerous journals and publications and were featured on *The Writer's Almanac* with Garrison Keillor. She is a member of Blue Roses Productions and the Dramatists' Guild of America. www.arlitia.com.

JASON. All hockey gear, everything on that wall is 20% off.

SHAUN. Thanks.

(beat)

JASON. You watch that game last night?

SHAUN. Uh, no. Didn't know there was a game.

JASON. Best game of the season.

SHAUN. (pause) I don't know what season this is.

JASON. Basketball.

SHAUN. Oh.

(beat)

JASON. Something I can help you with?

SHAUN. I need a uniform.

JASON. Baseball?

SHAUN. Football. Do you have a section for football?

JASON. I don't have anything to fit you.

SHAUN. Not me. (beat) (voice strained) My son. (stronger) I want to buy my son a football uniform.

JASON. He playing this fall?

SHAUN. No.

JASON. Summer training camp?

SHAUN. No.

JASON. What size is he?

SHAUN. Small. Skinny. Real skinny.

JASON. Mother had an affair with a pencil, one of those?

SHAUN. (small laugh)

JASON. How old is he?

SHAUN. (pause) Eight. Almost nine.

JASON. What's he weigh?

SHAUN. 67 pounds.

JASON. And that's if you put a rock in his pocket? He's the kicker, right?

SHAUN. *(laugh)* Probably.

JASON. What team?

SHAUN. Uhm. I'm not sure.

JASON. Is he with Pop Warner, or Boys and Girls Club?

SHAUN. Does it matter?

JASON. Is he on a team?

SHAUN. No.

(beat)

JASON. Does he even play football?

SHAUN. No. I just want to buy him a uniform. Can I do that?

JASON. Sure. You can buy whatever you want. I'm just sorry to see parents spend all their money on something their kids are gonna hate two months down the road.

SHAUN. He's not going to hate it.

JASON. My kid swore up and down he wanted to play hockey until came to actually getting in the car to go the rink for practice. Parents get their heart set on a kid playing and the kids' got other –

SHAUN. – I don't have my heart set on anything. I just want to buy him a uniform.

(beat)

JASON. You want to pick a team?

SHAUN. Yeah. A good one. Something cool.

JASON. I got Tigers and Bears, Lions and Devils.

SHAUN. Yeah?

JASON. Sharks. Stingrays. Storms. Hurricanes? I got a kid on the Hurricanes.

SHAUN. You got Tornadoes?

JASON. I got Tornadoes.

SHAUN. They any good? I want him to have a good team.

JASON. Pretty good. Went to finals last year. Lost in the first round. Coach called the wrong play, and threw the whole game, in my opinion. They should have won. They had some good kids, actually knew how to scrimmage. Pretty good for that age group.

SHAUN. Corey's a tough kid.

JASON. Then I guess he's a Tornado. You feel sorry for some of these kids, they actually got talent and they get on a bad team, playing with a bunch of spastics. They don't get to progress. They lose every game. It ain't fair.

(beat)

SHAUN. I took him cross-country to see his grandparents one time in Nebraska. He was four. And we got in this horrible storm. Tornado touched down about a half mile to the right of us. Just traveling along beside us like it knew where we were going. Corey was glued to the window. "Hey Daddy, what's that cloud doing?" It's spinning nine hundred miles an hour. We better get out of here before it comes this way. He didn't say anything for a minute. Just sat there watching it. His eyes barely see up over the car door. And then he said, "It'll get dizzy and fall over." That's what he said.

JASON. Funny.

SHAUN. It was. Out in the middle of nowhere, just me and my little son in the back seat. One of the most destructive forces on the planet spinning along on the other side of him. You know I'm looking at the ol' La Sabre thinking I hope it's got enough ponies under that hood to outrun this thing. Come on, Buick. Pedal to the metal. I got my foot sticking out the front grill, I'm mashing that throttle so hard. His mother would've killed me, if she'd known I had him out there.

JASON. She know you're letting him play football?

SHAUN. No. She doesn't know.

    (beat)

    Damn woman. I don't want him …*(His voice breaks into a sudden sob.)*

    (An awkward moment passes. **SHAUN** *is trying to compose himself.)*

JASON. I'll show you the logo.

SHAUN. Yeah. Ok. Let me see the logo.

JASON. It's a cool one.

SHAUN. Yeah?

    (**JASON** *produces a ball cap with a tornado logo on it.)*

JASON. Yeah. See. Got the Tornado. Dust clouds. Lightning bolt. Things laid to waste all around it.

SHAUN. I like that. It'd be cool if you could stitch a little Buick right here.

JASON. We could probably do that. Just have to put the graphic into the machine. Got red lettering, outlined in black and white.

SHAUN. Yeah, I like that. I'll take one of these ball caps. Two. Make that two. You got one that'll fit me?

JASON. Oh yeah. What number you want on his jersey?

SHAUN. 72.

JASON. That's a lineman's number.

SHAUN. That was my number.

JASON. You play highschool?

SHAUN. And college.

JASON. Where at?

SHAUN. Husker.

JASON. No shit? When'd you play?

SHAUN. 84 through 87.

JASON. I probably saw you play. What's your name?

SHAUN. Locker. Shaun Locker.

JASON. The Meat Locker! That was you, wasn't it? I remember you.

SHAUN. Yeah, that was me.

JASON. I always thought you'd go to the NFL.

SHAUN. I went to graduate school.

JASON. What do you do now?

SHAUN. Design airplanes.

JASON. No kidding. How come, if you're the designer, the seats are so small?

SHAUN. They don't let me design the seats. Just the ailerons.

JASON. You work for Boeing?

SHAUN. I did work for Boeing.

JASON. You and three thousand other people. *(beat)* Hey you need a ball with this uniform?

SHAUN. Yeah, I need a ball! He's got one at home, but it's pretty beat up.

JASON. One pigskin. You got it. Where you guys from?

SHAUN. Everett.

JASON. Oh. You in Seattle on a visit.

SHAUN. No. We live here. *(beat)* We've been staying over at the university hospital.

JASON. Oh. *(beat)* Hey I'll get you a kicker's tee too, so you don't have hold it for him all the time.

SHAUN. No, I don't need that. *(emotions overcoming him again)* Just the ball.

JASON. Ok.

(A moment passes as JASON retrieves the ball and SHAUN tries to recollect himself.)

JASON. Go long.

(JASON pumps the ball a couple times at SHAUN then tosses it. SHAUN pantomimes a great grab and tuck.)

SHAUN. Thanks. Oh, you probably need my credit card. Pay for all this.

JASON. Works for me.

(SHAUN *hands* JASON *his credit card.* JASON *removes to a location on stage where the cash register is located.*)

JASON. Thanks. I'll get your receipt.

(SHAUN *stands for a minute playing with the ball. He starts to pantomime throwing it to an invisible partner, but this upsets him. He stops the motion and stands holding the ball staring at it.*)

SHAUN. Used to play football all the time with my old man. Always tossing a ball. One time we were playing a game, me and my friends, and him. Kids against the old guy. Dad gets the ball and takes off running. We're playing out in the road in front of our house. Wannamaker's driveway is the goal line. He's got a clear shot. He's barreling down that road. Knocking kids left and right. Mowing us down. I jumped square in front of him to tackle and he ran through me like warm butter. Sent me flying, ass over teakettle, and when I finally quit spinning long enough to see what's going on, there's my dad, running. He's got his arm out, his head back and his legs pumping, all out, fast as he can go. He's twenty feet away from a touchdown and I hear this little pop sound. (*makes a pop with his mouth*) This ungodly scream comes out of my dad and he starts to fall. One hand holding that football, the other hand reaching back and grabbing his ass. Down he goes. Blew his hamstring. 20 feet from the goal line. He's writhing, grabbing his ass and we're all laughing so hard, laying there in the dirt where he knocked us down. Then I remember him stretching out, for all he's worth, that hand holding the football trying to get it past Wannamaker's driveway. He wasn't gonna give up.

(JASON *has come back during the preceding story. As* SHAUN *finishes a silence falls between them for a moment.*)

He's gone. He's gone, so I'm gone.

JASON. Your father?

SHAUN. *(Pause)* My son. Corey. He's gone.

JASON. I'm sorry.

SHAUN. Acute Lymphoblastic Leukemia. Sick most his life. Never got to play football with him, you know? Always too sick. *(pause)* We have to bury him in two days and I want to buy him his first football uniform. You have kids?

JASON. Yeah. Two boys.

SHAUN. Then you know. You know how much.

JASON. Yeah. I know.

SHAUN. I got up this morning and thought I need to get to the hospital. It's like he's still laying in that bed, and I'm there beside him and I just want to tear the room apart and smash myself against a wall. Then I remembered he isn't there anymore. Now all I can think to do is buy him his first football uniform so I can bury him in it and his mom won't put him in a goddamn suit which he would've hated.

(beat)

JASON. Mr. Locker. I'm sorry. Your card was declined.

SHAUN. What?

JASON. I'm sorry, I ran it twice.

*(An awkward moment passes. **SHAUN** takes his card back.)*

SHAUN. *(broken)* I'm sorry. *(beat)* I've been out of work.

*(***SHAUN** slowly gives the football back to **JASON**.)*

JASON. I'm sure it's just a misunderstanding with the bank. Why don't I hang on to this –

SHAUN. – No. Put it back. I'm sorry you went through all the trouble.

JASON. I don't mind. Really, I'll just put it all under the counter –

(**SHAUN** *suddenly searches in his pockets, empties them of all available cash.*)

SHAUN. – Wait a minute! How much for those caps?

JASON. Ten bucks.

SHAUN. *(disappointed)* A piece?

JASON. Here, why don't you take them. I don't need money.

SHAUN. No. I want to pay. I want to buy my son a cap. I want to do that. I got 14.

JASON. I'll take ten.

(**SHAUN** *pays him and dons the cap.*)

SHAUN. Thanks. How's it look?

JASON. Touchdown Tornado.

SHAUN. The crowd goes wild.

JASON. They're a good team.

End of Play

CPSIA information can be obtained at www.ICGtesting.com
Printed in the USA
LVOW10s0000241014

410312LV00012B/165/P